TAKE A BOOK
Little Free Library
RETURN A BOOK

·Jigsaw Pony·

BY JESSIE HAAS

PICTURES BY YING-HWA HU

Greenwillow Books
An Imprint of HarperCollinsPublishers

Jigsaw Pony
Text copyright © 2005 by Jessie Haas
Illustrations copyright © 2005 by Ying-Hwa Wu
All rights reserved. Printed in U.S.A.
www.harperchildrens.com

The text of this book is set in Schneidler.
Book design by Sylvie Le Floc'h.

Library of Congress Cataloging-in-Publication Data
Haas, Jessie.
Jigsaw Pony / by Jessie Haas;
pictures by Ying-Hwa Hu.
      p.   cm.
"Greenwillow Books."
Summary: Twins Kiera and Fran have never agreed on anything
but when their dream comes true and their father surprises
them with a pony, they must learn to work together to care
for their new pet.
ISBN 0-06-078245-5 (trade). ISBN 0-06-078250-1 (lib. bdg.)
[1. Ponies—Fiction. 2. Horses—Fiction. 3. Twins—Fiction.
4. Cooperativeness—Fiction. 5. Responsibility—Fiction.]
I. Hu, Ying-Hwa, ill. II. Title.
PZ7.H11133Ji 2005   [E]—dc22   2004060724

First Edition 10 9 8 7 6 5

[[Greenwillow Books logo]] Greenwillow Books

For the real Shaws,
Jean & Gay
—J. H.

To my mother,
who inspires me
—Y. H.

~CONTENTS~

CHAPTER ONE
Jigsaw

When Jigsaw had Valerie nearly
trained, she moved away.

Jigsaw was an old pony by then.

Valerie was his fourth girl.

The other three were grown-ups

now. They had pictures on their walls of Jigsaw, with horse show ribbons, with Christmas wreaths. Pictures of them hugging him. Pictures in heart-shaped frames.

But Jigsaw had not seen any of them in years. Now Valerie was gone, too, so far away that her letters took a week to come. Jigsaw lived in a big weedy pasture on a lonely hill. Next to the pasture lived Valerie's grandmother, in a lonely house.

The grandmother watched Jigsaw out her window. She was lame. She rode an electric cart to the mailbox to get Valerie's letters.

The mailbox was at the bottom of the pasture. Jigsaw often met Valerie's grandmother there, but she couldn't pat him. There was a ditch next to the fence. The cart couldn't cross it.

"What am I going to do with you, Jig?" the grandmother asked. "I can't take care of you. I can barely take care of myself."

Jigsaw had no answer. But as the days passed, the grandmother watching out her window noticed something.

Early every afternoon Jigsaw lifted his head. He pointed his ears toward the road and listened.

Then he trotted down through the weeds. He dodged the thistles. He hopped over the fallen log and got to the mailbox just as the mailman did.

The mailman parked his car. He took the grandmother's letter out of the box. He put Valerie's postcard in.

Next he pulled an apple from his pocket. He hopped across the ditch and gave the apple to Jigsaw.

Crunch munch slobber—Jigsaw

ate the apple quickly. He reached over the fence again. He and the mailman sniffed noses.

"Poor little guy," the mailman said. "Who takes care of you?" He looked up at the house, but he never saw anyone.

One day when Jigsaw and the mailman were sniffing noses, the mailman said, "Oh, look at you!"

Big brown burrs were stuck to Jigsaw's sides. His mane was matted together. His tail looked like a fat brown stick.

The burrs were itchy. Normally Jigsaw didn't go near them. But the rest of the grass was eaten down short. Jigsaw had to eat where the burrs grew or go hungry.

The mailman—his name was Mr. Shaw—looked around. Nobody was in sight. He ducked under the fence and started pulling burrs.

They came off Jigsaw's sides easily enough. But burrs don't come out of a pony's mane without a struggle. Mr. Shaw looked at his watch. He had to get back to the post office soon.

Scritch scritch, went the burrs.

"Sorry," Mr. Shaw said. "Does this—"

"Hello!" said a voice behind him.

Mr. Shaw jumped and turned. There sat Valerie's grandmother in her cart.

"Sorry," he said. "I shouldn't be in your—"

"I've seen you feeding him," the grandmother said. She had to move slowly, but she spoke quickly and didn't always let people finish their sentences. "I keep trying to get down to talk to you, but you leave too fast!"

"I hope you don't mind," Mr. Shaw said. "He seems lo—"

"He is lonely," said Valerie's grandmother. "There's no one to ride him anymore. Do you want him?"

"I—" said Mr. Shaw.

"He gets grass here, but that's about it. A pony needs more care than that. Anyway, winter's coming." Really, winter was months away, but Valerie's grandmother was right. Sooner or later it would come.

"Do you have children?" she asked.

"As a matter of fact," Mr. Shaw said,

"I have twin girls. Kiera and Fran. They tell me our yard is big enough for a pony. It's the only thing they've ever agreed on."

"Then it's settled," said Valerie's grandmother. "I'll give you his saddle and bridle, and you can take him home."

"But—" said Mr. Shaw. "But *how*? I don't have a horse trailer."

"He'll hop right in your backseat. Jigsaw can do anything."

That was true, but the grandmother wasn't perfectly sure Jigsaw would get into a car. She held her chin high and hoped for the best.

Mr. Shaw looked at Jigsaw. What should he do? He liked this pony. Fran and Kiera would like him, too. But there would be problems. Lots and lots of problems.

Maybe he won't get in, Mr. Shaw thought. He led Jigsaw to the car and opened the back door.

"Up you go, Jig," said Valerie's grandmother.

Jigsaw had never been in a car. Most ponies haven't. But he liked trying new things, and he liked Mr. Shaw.

He put his front feet in.

"Give him a boost," the grandmother said.

Mr. Shaw pushed against Jigsaw's rump. Jigsaw scrambled into the car. He leaned against the backseat. Then he lay down on it. He sniffed the mailbags.

"Don't eat those!" Mr. Shaw said. He was nervous. He'd never had a pony in his car before. It was probably against post office rules.

CHAPTER TWO

Kiera and Fran

If it was against the rules to have
a pony in the car, nobody at the post
office cared. Everyone rushed out
to see.

A policeman brought Jigsaw a

doughnut. A lady got him a carrot from her grocery bag. The postmaster gave Jigsaw a drink.

"Kiera and Fran are going to love him," the postmaster said.

Kiera and Fran are going to fight about him, Mr. Shaw thought. But he didn't say that. He got back in the car and drove Jigsaw home.

When Mrs. Shaw saw Jigsaw, she said, "I had a feeling you'd bring that pony home. Girls! Come see what your father's got."

Kiera ran from the bedroom. Fran ran from the tree house.

"A *pony*!" they both said at exactly the same time. Usually they hated when that happened. This time they didn't even notice.

"He's *beautiful*!" Kiera said.

"He's *darling*!" Fran said.

"He's on our backseat," their mother said. "Don't you think we'd better get him out?"

Mr. Shaw helped Jigsaw out of the car.

"Oh, Daddy, he's covered with burrs!" Kiera said.

"Daddy, he's starving," Fran said.

"Not quite starving, but he is hungry," their father said.

Already Jigsaw was eating the lawn. Rip, rip, rip, went his teeth. A good green smell came up from the grass. It went with the good green taste in Jigsaw's mouth.

While he ate, Jigsaw looked around. He saw a garden shed and apple trees. He saw a big yard. He saw Fran and Kiera. Two girls, just the right age.

That was as good as the grass. Jigsaw's neck had missed hugs. Now someone was hugging him. His ears had missed kisses. Now someone was kissing him. Someone patted him. Someone took burrs out of his tail. Jigsaw was an expert on girls. He knew these were good ones.

Mr. and Mrs. Shaw stood back. "Amazing!" Mr. Shaw whispered. "They're not—"

"*Shh!*" Mrs. Shaw said. "They will."

But right then Kiera and Fran weren't worried about having to share. They weren't worried about taking turns. Their dream had come true: their own pony, in their own yard, eating their lawn.

He was just the right color, too.

"Thank you, Daddy!" Kiera hugged Mr. Shaw. "I've *always* wanted a white pony."

Fran was shocked. "He isn't white! He's *black*, the perfect color for a pony."

"He's a white pony with black

patches," Kiera said. "Anybody can see that!"

"He's black with white blotches," Fran said. "It's obvious!"

"He's nothing of the kind," said their father. "Exactly half of him is white. Exactly half of him is black. I searched everywhere for a pony like this, because I knew you'd fight about it."

Kiera and Fran looked at their father. "That's not true, is it, Daddy?" Fran said.

"This is the pony you've been

bringing apples to, isn't he, Daddy?"
Kiera said. "You were going to take us
to see him someday."

"This is that pony," their father
said. "His name is Jigsaw."

Fran and Kiera didn't need to look
at each other. Each knew at once that
Jigsaw was not the perfect name for
her pony.

"Midnight," Fran said. "Look, his
eyelashes are black."

"Snowflake," Kiera said. "His
whiskers are white."

Their mother said, "He's a black-

and-white pony. A black-and-white pony with no stall and no pasture fence. I think someone needs to do something about that."

CHAPTER THREE

Jody

Kiera and Fran went with their father to the feed store.

It was hard to leave Jigsaw, even for a minute, but Mr. Shaw didn't know what to buy. Kiera and Fran did. They'd wanted a pony for a long time. They'd wanted all the things a pony needs, too.

Ponies need a lot. By the time Fran and Kiera were through shopping, there was a huge pile to go into the car.

Fence posts.

Fence wire.

An electric fence charger.

Hay.

A water pail.

Grain.

A grain pail.

Shavings.

A shovel.

A rake.

Fly spray.

A lead rope.

A hoof pick.

Two brushes.

A mane comb.

A salt brick.

Saddle soap.

And two kinds of shampoo.

"I didn't know ponies needed shampoo," their father said. "Can we put one back?"

"He's mostly black," Fran said. "He needs black pony shampoo."

"Actually, he's mostly white," Kiera said. "So he needs white pony shampoo."

"Can't he just borrow some of mine?" their father asked.

"Daddy!" Fran said.

"Don't say *Daddy* to Daddy!" Kiera said.

"Fine," their father said. "Two kinds of shampoo."

"It must be wonderful to be twins!" the feed store lady said. "You'd never be lonely."

Fran and Kiera pretended not to hear her.

Back home Mrs. Shaw held Jigsaw's rope. She watched him eat grass. She listened to the sound of his teeth.

"Wow!" somebody said behind her. "A pony!"

It was Jody, Fran and Kiera's friend from down the street.

"Yes," Mrs. Shaw said. "Jody, meet Jigsaw."

always wanted a pony. Maybe they'll finally learn to share."

Jody didn't answer. But she thought Mrs. Shaw was wrong.

Jody was Fran's best friend. She was Kiera's best friend, too. She knew how hard it was to be twins because Fran and Kiera told her.

Nobody remembers who's the oldest—Fran—or the youngest—Kiera. People think they can tell you apart. They're wrong. Someone is always finishing your sentences, or starting them.

Jody patted Jigsaw's neck. She found more burrs and started to take them out.

Another girl. Another good one. To Jigsaw, this seemed like a very nice neighborhood.

"What a great name!" Jody said. "His black parts and his white parts fit together like a puzzle."

"Yes," Mrs. Shaw said. "But they don't come apart like a puzzle."

Jody asked, "Are they—"

Mrs. Shaw nodded. "But they've

And even though you're very different—as different as black and white—lots of times you like the same things. The more you like them, the harder it is to share. That was true about jelly beans. It was true about Jody. It was going to be true about Jigsaw.

"But they're *great*," Jody whispered in Jigsaw's ear. "You'll love them both, and they'll love you."

Jigsaw rubbed his head against Jody. Hugs. Kisses. Whispers. He loved all the girls he'd met today.

The car pulled in, and two voices said, "I'm calling Jody!"

"No, *I'm* calling her!"

"Calling me what?" Jody asked. "I just met Jigsaw!"

"Midnight," said Fran.

"Snowflake," said Kiera.

Jody said, "I love his brown eyes."

"Me too," Kiera and Fran said together.

For the rest of the afternoon everyone, including Jody, worked hard. They took turns holding Jigsaw's lead rope and letting him

eat the lawn. They put up fence posts. They put up wire. They took the garden tools out of the shed. They turned it into a stall, and they put in shavings.

The sun went down. Jody went home. Just as it was getting dark, Fran and Kiera led Jigsaw inside the shed. They gave him hay and water and closed the door.

After supper their mother said, "It's been a big day, girls. Time for bed."

"I want to say good night to Snowflake."

"I want to say good night to Midnight."

"Go ahead," said their father.

"But—" said Kiera.

"I wanted—" said Fran.

They looked at their plates. More than anything, Fran wanted time alone with Midnight. More than anything, Kiera wanted time alone with Snowflake. But only one of them could have that. They would have to take turns.

Kiera and Fran *hated* taking turns.

"I understand," their mother said. "I really do understand." She reached for the two sticks of spaghetti she always kept handy. "Whoever picks the long spaghetti goes out tonight."

Kiera and Fran each chose a spaghetti. Kiera got the long one. "Hurray!" She took the flashlight and an apple and ran outside.

"I'm sorry, Fran," Mrs. Shaw said. "Tomorrow night it's your turn."

"I know," Fran said. She was already marking it on the calendar.

Kiera crossed the dark yard. She opened the stall door. "Hi, Snowflake."

Jigsaw made a rumbling sound. He was glad to see Kiera and glad to see the apple, too. He reached for it. Crunch munch slobber.

When it was gone, Jigsaw lifted his nose to Kiera's face. Kiera smelled apple and sweet pony breath. A shiver went down her back. This was just the way she'd always thought it would be.

CHAPTER FOUR

Charts

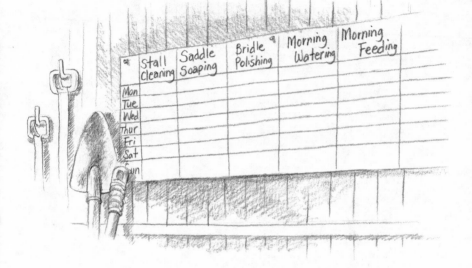

Fran woke early the next morning.
She tiptoed out of the room. The door
banged behind her.

"No fair!" Kiera said before her eyes
were even open. She raced downstairs.

But Fran got to the stall first.
Jigsaw was glad to see her. He made
a rumbling sound. He lifted his nose
to Fran's face. She smelled hay and
sweet pony breath. It made her
shiver. All night she'd dreamed of
this. Now her dream had come true.

Kiera came through the door.
Behind her came their father. "I
brought Jig some water."

"He's our pony!" Kiera said.

"We should take care of him," Fran
said.

Mr. Shaw said, "I thought it might

be hard for you to get everything done before school."

"School?"

"School?"

Kiera and Fran had forgotten about school. It seemed silly to go to school when they had a pony in their backyard for the first time ever.

"I have to clean Snowflake's stall."

"*I* was going to clean *Midnight*'s stall."

"I've always wanted to clean my own pony's stall."

"No fair! You went out first last

night. I should get to clean the stall first."

"Fran is right," their mother said. "She will clean the stall—after school."

"Then who gets to feed him first?"

Mrs. Shaw looked tired, even though it was only morning. "I'll draw up a chart," she said. "We'll work it all out. *After school!*"

All day Kiera drew pictures of Snowflake. Fran wrote poems to Midnight. Jody stared into space and thought about Jigsaw.

After school they ran home. "Go change your clothes, Jody," Fran said.

"We'll ride," Kiera said.

They all had taken riding lessons at Tish's camp on a little red pony named Radish. Radish was a *good* bad pony. He *could* behave, but he wouldn't—not until his riders learned how to make him.

Jigsaw wasn't like that.

"Wow!" said Jody. "He picks his feet up before I even ask. He *wants* me to clean them out."

"He doesn't fill himself up with air

when I tighten the girth," Kiera said. "I think he *likes* being saddled."

"He just *reached* for the bit," said Fran. "He almost put the bridle on himself."

There was only one thing Jigsaw couldn't make easy. He couldn't decide who would ride first.

More than anything, Kiera wanted it to be her. More than anything, Fran wanted it to be *her*. It was the same problem they always had with important things, only this was worse.

They didn't want to choose spaghetti. They didn't want to do Rock Paper Scissors. They didn't even want to argue, which was unusual. It was so wonderful to have a pony that arguing didn't seem right. But someone did have to ride first.

Fran and Kiera looked at Jody. She was kissing Jigsaw's nose.

"Oh!" Fran said. She was good at thinking up ideas. "I know!"

"Yes," Kiera said. She always understood Fran's ideas, almost as quickly as Fran did.

They both said, "You go first, Jody."

"But he's not my pony!" Jody said.

"Yes, he is," Fran said.

"We're sharing him with you," Kiera said.

"So you ride first," they both said.

Jody got on Jigsaw. She rode him around the pasture. She was a good rider, Jigsaw could tell. She knew how to hang on tight. She knew how to ask a pony to do things. She was firm but not pushy.

Kiera and Fran chose spaghetti. Then they took their turns. They were good riders, too, and more polite than Jigsaw had expected.

Fran asked Jigsaw to canter. He did. Kiera asked him to jump over a stick. He did that, too. He was pleased with them, and they were pleased with him.

But the rides had to be short. There was a lot of work to do.

Fran cleaned the stall and wheeled the wheelbarrow to the compost pile and spread shavings. Jody helped her.

Kiera filled the water bucket.

"I was going to do that," Fran said. "It's part of stall cleaning."

"No, it's part of feeding. If you get to clean the stall, I get to feed."

Mrs. Shaw stopped picking tomatoes. "Chart time!" She tacked a big piece of paper to the shed wall. Jody went into the pasture with Jigsaw. She always stayed out of the way when Fran and Kiera were making charts.

Kiera and Fran divided the chores.

Stall cleaning.

Saddle soaping.

Bridle polishing.

They divided morning watering and night watering. Morning feeding and night feeding. Letting Jigsaw out of his stall. Putting him in again. One twin got to kiss Jigsaw good night. The other got to go out first in the morning. Everything Fran did one day, Kiera did the next. And the other way around.

"And on the days *I* go out first," Kiera said, "I'll put my nameplate on the door. I made it in art."

"Snowflake," said the nameplate, in flowing blue letters.

"On the days when *I* go out first," Fran said, "*my* nameplate goes on the door!" "Midnight," this nameplate said, in glowing red letters.

Mrs. Shaw wrote that on the chart. She had to write small. There was hardly any room.

It looked as if they were done. Jody came back just as Fran said, "Now we need a riding chart."

Mrs. Shaw said, "Can't you just take turns?"

"There are three of us," Fran said. "So the turns have to be really short."

"I don't have to ride," Jody said. "He's not my po—"

Fran and Kiera looked hard at her. Jody stopped talking.

Fran said, "Every day two of us can take short rides—"

"I get it!" Kiera said. "And one can take a long ride."

"Who gets the first long ride?" Fran asked.

Mrs. Shaw reached for the spaghetti.

CHAPTER FIVE

Barrel Racing

Fran chose the long spaghetti.

The next afternoon Kiera and Jody

took turns riding Jigsaw up and

down the street.

Meanwhile Fran borrowed both

garbage cans. She borrowed the umbrella stand. She set them up in a big triangle in the pasture.

"What are you doing?" Mrs. Shaw asked.

"Barrel racing," Fran said. "You ride around the barrels in a cloverleaf as fast as you can. I did it at camp. Radish was the fastest."

"Jigsaw will be fast, too," Jody said.

Fran got on Jigsaw. She rode to the starting line. She grabbed a handful of his mane. Jody said, *"Go!"*

Jigsaw galloped toward the first garbage can. His hooves thundered, and his mane flew. Fran held on tight. It was just like riding Radish, just like riding in a real barrel race.

Jigsaw whirled around the garbage can. He started toward the umbrella stand. He was slowing down. Fran nudged him with her heels.

Jigsaw went slower.

He trotted around the umbrella stand. He headed for the second garbage can. Now he was jogging very slowly.

"Giddup!" Fran said. "Go! *Canter!*"
She kicked Jigsaw's sides.

Jigsaw didn't go one bit faster. He
headed straight toward the garbage
can. His ears pointed forward. He
looked cheerful, and he was cheerful.
But he kept slowing down.

When Radish wouldn't go, Tish
used to say, "Smack him with your
whip!"

But when Radish wouldn't go,
he was being naughty. Jigsaw was
being good. At least that was how
it seemed to Fran. She knew she

could never smack him with a whip.

Kiera and Jody were watching. They would think she wasn't a good rider.

So Fran slowed Jigsaw down even more. "Walk," she said, and patted his neck. "Good boy! Thank you! That was enough for the first time."

Kiera and Jody didn't say anything.

That night Fran piled all the pony books on her bed. She got her flashlight. She turned off her lamp and pulled the covers over her head.

Kiera turned off her lamp, too. A

tiny glow of light came through
Fran's covers. A tiny whispering
sound came every time Fran turned
a page.

Kiera knew what Fran was doing.
It was just what *she* would have been
doing. Fran was trying to figure out
how to make Jigsaw keep going fast.

When they were younger, Kiera
would have said, "We're *supposed* to
be sleeping!" She would have said it
loud enough for their parents to
hear.

Now she didn't feel like doing that. She lay in bed watching the light until she fell asleep.

At breakfast Fran said, "We should have a blacksmith come."

"Is something wrong with Jigsaw's feet?" Mr. Shaw asked.

"I don't know," Fran said. "But the blacksmith should come every six weeks. That's what the books say. If you ride a pony when his feet aren't trimmed, you can hurt him."

"Better not ride then," Mr. Shaw said.

Mrs. Shaw looked in the phone book. "There are three blacksmiths. Who should we call?"

Mr. Shaw said, "I know who to ask."

When Mr. Shaw got to the grandmother's mailbox, he stepped out of his car. He waited. In a minute he saw the electric cart start down the driveway.

As soon as she was close enough, Valerie's grandmother said, "I need to talk to you. Valerie's upset that I gave away her pony."

Mr. Shaw said, "I hope she doesn't want him—"

"She's moved to Australia! Too far to take a pony. But she would like to hear from him. Here's her address."

Mr. Shaw said, "I'll have him write."

"I'm sure he could," said Valerie's grandmother. "But while he's learning, your girls can write for him. Are they taking good—"

"They fight about who gets to

clean his stall," said Mr. Shaw. "They fight about who gets to lug the water bucket. The only time *I* get to do anything for him is after they've gone to bed."

"I'm glad to hear it," said Valerie's grandmother.

The best blacksmith, the grandmother said, was Mr. Fletcher. He promised to come next week.

That was a long time not to ride, but Kiera, Fran, and Jody were too busy to mind much. They brushed

Jigsaw. They combed his mane and tail. They played games with him—Jigsaw was the horse—and shared their snacks.

Kiera and Fran wrote postcards to Valerie. "Jigsaw is the best pony ever," Kiera wrote. "Did you know he likes bananas?"

"How did you make Jigsaw go fast?" Fran wrote. "Does he like barrel racing? Or not?"

CHAPTER SIX

Show-and-Tell

"Fran. Kiera. Jody."

It was the middle of the next week.

Mrs. Ramsey, their teacher, looked at

them sternly.

"This is a beautiful picture of a

pony jumping. This is a fantastic
picture of a pony barrel racing. I love
this picture of a pony in the
backseat of a car. But you're in
school. You're supposed to be doing
schoolwork."

Kiera said, "Thank you." Jody and
Fran turned red.

Mrs. Ramsey said, "What can I do
to help you three pay attention?"

"Let us bring our pony in?" Kiera
said. The class laughed.

But Mrs. Ramsey said, "All right.
Bring him in for show-and-tell. Just

have someone come along to walk him back home."

That afternoon Fran, Kiera, and Jody got out both kinds of shampoo. They got buckets and sponges and warm water. They washed Jigsaw. They dried him in the sun. They dried him with the hair dryer. They filled his stall with clean, fresh shavings, so he couldn't get dirty overnight. In the morning they got up early to brush him. Jody came over to help.

"He's so white," Mrs. Shaw said. "Dazzling!"

"And so black," Mr. Shaw said. "Inky!"

They started to school. Mrs. Shaw went, too, to bring Jigsaw back.

Neighbors came out. "Where are you all going with that pony?"

When they heard, the neighbors told stories about things *they'd* taken to show-and-tell.

"But never a pony."

"Right into the classroom?"

"Mrs. Ramsey says yes," Fran said.

When they got to school, no one was on the playground. "Hurry," Kiera said. "Everyone's gone inside."

At the front steps Mrs. Shaw asked, "Can ponies climb stairs?"

"Jigsaw can," Jody said.

Jigsaw had never climbed stairs before. Most ponies haven't. But he'd climbed lots of rocky hills. The school stairs looked easy, and they were. Jody and Mrs. Shaw held open the big doors. Fran and Kiera led Jigsaw inside.

"Don't we need to stop at the office?" Mrs. Shaw asked. "Don't we need to see the principal?"

"No," Jody said. "Mrs. Ramsey said bring him in."

They walked down the hall. *Ca-lip ca-lop ca-lippity-clop*, went Jigsaw's feet on the hard floor. Heads popped out of classrooms. The principal's door opened.

They walked into Mrs. Ramsey's classroom.

Mrs. Ramsey was taking attendance. "Fran Shaw, not here? Kiera Shaw—oh, my goodness!"

"Are we early for show-and-tell?" Kiera asked.

Mrs. Ramsey shook her head. "N-no. But I thought you'd bring him to the playground. I thought the class would come outside to meet him."

Kiera and Fran looked at each other. "Well, he's here now," Kiera said.

"So, can he stay?" Fran asked.

"I . . . guess so," Mrs. Ramsey said. "Come right up to the front of the room!"

Fran and Kiera led Jigsaw up between the desks. Jody went with them. Mrs. Shaw stood back to watch.

Jigsaw looked bigger here than he did outdoors. He made the classroom seem small and crowded. One or two people looked scared.

Not Jigsaw. He tasted a blackboard eraser. It wasn't good. Chalk wasn't good either.

The principal came in. "I *thought*
I saw a pony going down the hall!"

"He's here for show-and-tell," said
Mrs. Ramsey. "I hope that's all right."

"It's certainly a first," the principal
said.

"Class," Mrs. Ramsey said, "raise
your hands if you'd like to ask Kiera
and Fran a question about their
pony."

A lot of hands went up. Six people
asked, "What's his name?"

Fran and Kiera looked at each

other. Fran wanted to say Midnight. Kiera wanted to say Snowflake. But they knew their friends would ask, "Don't you know your own pony's name?" And later they'd say, "Boy, the Shaw twins fight about *everything*!"

"Jigsaw," they both said together. "His name is Jigsaw."

There were lots more questions. "What does he eat?" "Does he bite? Or kick?" "Can I ride him?" "Can *I*?"

"*We* don't even ride him yet," Kiera said.

"We're waiting for the blacksmith," Fran said.

Now people came up two by two to pat Jigsaw.

"I love his long whiskers!"

"I love his eyes."

"His ears are so cute!"

"He's been a wonderful guest," Mrs. Ramsey said at last. "Thank you for visiting, Jigsaw."

Mrs. Shaw led Jigsaw out of the

classroom. They stopped in the hall so the principal could pat him, too. Jigsaw tasted some of the art on the walls. It was rather dry.

"I don't suppose he'd like an apple?" the principal asked. "I brought one with my lunch."

While Jigsaw was eating the principal's apple, Mrs. Ramsey was trying to start the school day. "Fran, Kiera, and Jody are going to think about schoolwork now," she said. "And so is everybody else."

But for the rest of that day everyone in class thought mostly about Jigsaw.

CHAPTER SEVEN
Blacksmith

Mrs. Shaw enjoyed leading

Jigsaw home so much she started

taking him on her morning walks.

They met dogs on leashes. They

met babies in strollers. They met

people with canes, and people jogging, and everyone was surprised and pleased to see a pony.

Soon they started watching for him. They gave him apples, and carrots, and oatmeal raisin cookies.

On Saturday Mr. Fletcher came.

"Hello, Jig. Looks as if those feet need trimming."

He bent down. Jigsaw lifted his foot before Mr. Fletcher even touched it. But Mr. Fletcher said, *"Ow!"*

He straightened slowly. He put one hand on his back.

"Ponies are the hardest thing I do," he said. "Too far *down*!"

"Put him up on something," said Mr. Shaw. "What about the back of your truck?"

Mr. Fletcher laughed. "You don't know much about ponies, do you?"

Kiera and Fran looked at each other. That was true, but they didn't think Mr. Fletcher should say it.

"Daddy *doesn't* know much about ponies," Kiera said.

"But *we* do," Fran said.

"And *we* think it's a good idea," they said together.

Fran said, "Can you move your truck to where the sidewalk's high?"

Mr. Fletcher moved his truck. Fran and Kiera got into the back. Kiera held the rope. Fran had an apple.

"Up you go, Jig," said Mr. Shaw.

Jigsaw had never climbed into a pickup before. But it didn't look hard. Fran and Kiera were up there. So was the apple. He put his front feet on the tailgate.

"Help me give him a boost," said Mr. Shaw.

"Ow!" said Mr. Fletcher. With a scramble and a couple of thuds, Jigsaw landed in the back of the truck.

He ate the apple. Then he let Kiera and Fran lead him to the edge of the tailgate. He held up his foot for Mr. Fletcher.

"Perfect!" said Mr. Fletcher. "I don't have to bend a bit. Wish I'd thought of this years ago!"

Jigsaw looked across the front

yards. He could see a lot more from up this high. Cars slowed down on the street. Neighbors came out to watch.

"I *never* saw a pony do anything like that!"

"I never even saw a picture of one doing that!"

When Mr. Fletcher was through with both left feet, Fran and Kiera turned Jigsaw around. Now he looked at the houses across the street. That was interesting, too.

Mr. Fletcher finished trimming

Jigsaw's feet. "Okay, let's get him down."

Fran and Kiera got out of the truck. "Come on, Jig! Hop down."

Jigsaw looked at them. He was a long way up. Hopping down didn't look easy. It didn't look safe.

Jigsaw didn't move.

"Uh-oh," said Mr. Fletcher. "Now what?"

"It's too far down," said Mr. Shaw. For someone who didn't know much about ponies, he was a very good guesser. "We need a step, so it's easier for him."

"A wheelbarrow?" one neighbor asked.

"Too tippy," Fran said.

"What about my big plastic toolbox?" asked another neighbor.

"Not strong enough," Kiera said.

"There's a stump at the edge of our lawn," Jody said.

"Good idea," Fran said.

"He could use that for a step," Kiera said.

"I'll back up to it," Mr. Fletcher

said. "But somebody has to ride with him, and hold on tight. If he gets scared, he might jump out and hurt himself."

Mr. Shaw got up with Jigsaw. Mr. Fletcher started the truck. He backed so slowly that the truck hardly seemed to move. Fran, Kiera, Jody, and the neighbors walked alongside.

"Easy, Jigsaw!"

"It's okay."

"Don't be scared."

Jigsaw wasn't a bit scared. He'd been in horse trailers before. He'd ridden in a car. He watched the houses and yards creep past. He nuzzled Mr. Shaw's hand.

"I used to be your only friend," Mr. Shaw said. "Now you've got a whole neighborhood of friends."

Jigsaw lifted his head. He and Mr. Shaw sniffed noses, just like the old days. "You're a good little guy," Mr. Shaw said.

Mr. Fletcher stopped next to the big stump. Fran and Kiera stood on each side of it. Fran held Jigsaw's rope. Kiera said, "Come on, boy!"

Jigsaw looked at the stump. It was broad and flat and not very far down.

He stepped onto it with one round, trimmed hoof—then two, and three, and four. The neighbors cheered. Jigsaw stepped onto Jody's lawn. He tasted it.

More good grass. This really was a very nice neighborhood.

CHAPTER EIGHT

Jumping

The next day Kiera said, "It's my turn for the long ride."

Fran was glad. Jigsaw's feet had needed trimming. Mr. Fletcher said so. But he didn't seem shocked. He didn't say they were awful.

If Jigsaw's feet were okay, then maybe something was wrong with Fran. Maybe she wasn't a good rider.

So Fran was glad just to ride up and down the street. That was easy. Jody walked along.

Then Jody rode and Fran walked along. They met dogs they knew. Neighbors came out to say hi. The baby from two houses down squealed *ee-aw*!

"He said 'Jigsaw!'" the baby's mother said. "His first word!"

Back in the pasture Kiera was setting up jumps. She used old beanpoles from the garden. She propped them on rocks and buckets and hay bales. There were four jumps in all.

When Jigsaw came back, Kiera got on. She rode in a little circle. Then she asked Jigsaw to canter and pointed him at the jumps.

Jigsaw flew over the first jump

just the way Radish used to. Kiera felt as if she were in a real horse show. She felt as if she were about to win a blue ribbon.

Jigsaw landed on the other side of the jump. He cantered toward the second one. He was going slower. Kiera nudged him with her heels, but Jigsaw kept slowing down.

He leaped anyway, but he barely made it. Kiera heard his back feet rap the pole. He slowed to a trot.

He still looked happy, and he was happy. He trotted up to the third jump and pushed the beanpole with his nose.

It fell to the ground. Jigsaw trotted over it. He walked to the fourth jump. He pushed that beanpole off, too, and stepped carefully over it and stopped.

Kiera's face felt hot. She didn't look back at Fran and Jody. There was only one thing Kiera was glad of right now. She was very glad she hadn't teased Fran about the barrel racing.

That night Kiera piled all the pony books on her bed. She got her flashlight. She turned off her lamp and pulled the covers over her head.

Fran turned off her lamp, too. She looked across at Kiera's bed. A tiny light glowed under the covers. A tiny whisper of sound came every time Kiera turned a page.

Fran knew what Kiera was doing. She was doing the same thing Fran had done. She was trying to figure out how to make

Jigsaw do what she wanted.

When they were younger, Fran

would have said, "The flashlight's

keeping me awake!" She would have

said it loud enough for their parents

to hear. Now she didn't feel like

doing that. She lay in bed listening

to the pages whisper.

After a while Fran whispered, too.

"I don't think it's us. We're good

riders. Tish said so."

Under the covers, Kiera said, "If

it's not us, then something's wrong with Jigsaw. Maybe he's sick."

Fran took her flashlight over to Kiera's bed. She got under the covers and reached for a book. They both read until the flashlights were too dim to see by anymore.

At breakfast the next morning Kiera said, "We should have a vet come look at Jigsaw."

"Is something the matter with him?" Mr. Shaw asked.

"N-no," said Kiera.

"Maybe," Fran said. "He doesn't like to keep going fast."

"He doesn't like to keep jumping either," Kiera said.

"Are you sure you're riding him right?" Mr. Shaw asked.

"I hope not," Kiera said. Fran didn't say anything.

"Why don't you ask Tish to come?" Mrs. Shaw said. "She knows everything about ponies, and she knows how well you ride, too."

୬

When they called her, Tish said, "I'll be glad to come. How about Monday?"

Fran went to mark it on the calendar. "That's the day after Halloween!"

"*Halloween!*" Kiera said. "What are we going to *be*?"

Usually they spent weeks thinking about their costumes. They had to be exact opposites. A ballerina and an elephant. A vampire and an angel.

This year they'd been too busy to

think about costumes. They looked
out the window at Jigsaw.

Fran said, "What if we—"

Kiera said, "Perfect!"

CHAPTER NINE

Halloween

All week Kiera and Fran
worked on their costume.

First they chose spaghetti.
Then they chose fabric and
yarn. They sewed. They

practiced. Jody helped. So did Mrs. Shaw.

Jigsaw ate grass and crisp fall apples. He watched Mr. Shaw put the garden to bed. On frosty mornings the cat warmed her toes on his back. On bright afternoons he curled in the sun. Kiera, Fran, and Jody read him stories.

Jigsaw enjoyed that. He liked their quiet voices. He liked their leaning on him.

One day a letter came from Valerie. Kiera read it aloud.

"I was worried when Gram gave Jigsaw away," Valerie wrote. "She couldn't take care of him, but at least they had each other.

"Jigsaw has a good home now, but Gram is all by herself. I'm glad your father has tea with her sometimes and gets things off high shelves for her. Tell him thank you for fixing her stairs."

"I didn't know Daddy did that," Kiera said.

She read the rest of Valerie's letter. "I never asked Jigsaw to barrel race, so

I don't know if he likes it. We mostly took slow rides in the woods.

"Tell Jig I miss him. Tell Gram, too, if you see her."

"I'd *like* to see her," Fran said. "Let's ask her to the Halloween party."

Jigsaw sniffed the letter. It smelled like Valerie. He didn't miss Valerie. He was too happy. But her scent on the paper made him even happier.

Halloween night was warm and windy. Ghosts and dancers, spacemen and black cats walked up and down the street.

A cowgirl led two ponies from house to house. One pony had black and white patches that fitted together like a jigsaw puzzle.

The front half of the other pony was black. The back half was white.

The ponies came right up the steps of the houses. The neighbors said, "Hello, Jigsaw! And who is this pony?"

"Midnight," said the black head.

"Snowflake," said the white tail.

"It's a little confused," said the cowgirl. "Trick or treat!"

After trick-or-treating, the ponies and ghosts, dancers and spacemen walked to school for the Halloween party. Neighbors and parents went, too.

Mr. Shaw was already there with Valerie's grandmother. They watched the costume parade. Some of the costumes were scary, but neither pony seemed afraid.

When the parade was over, Jody—she was the cowgirl—brought her ponies across the gym.

"Hello, Jig," said Valerie's grandmother.

Jigsaw lifted his nose to her face. He blew his breath on her. "You smell like taffy apples," the grandmother said.

The other pony came apart. Fran was inside the black half. Kiera was inside the white half.

"*Thank* you," Fran said.

"For letting us have Jigsaw," Kiera said.

"Valerie told me I was hasty," said the grandmother. "I should have made sure you'd take good care of him. But I knew you would. Look at who your father is!"

"Jody helps," Fran said.

"This is Jody," Kiera said.

Valerie's grandmother said, "Three best friends."

"Four!" Jody put her arm around Jigsaw's neck.

Valerie's grandmother gave Jigsaw a kiss. "Go on, you four," she said. "Don't miss the games!"

They played Doughnut on a String. Jigsaw bit more doughnuts than anyone. He was the best at apple dunking, too.

Some kids were afraid to go through the Haunted House. Jigsaw went along to help them be brave. Fake cobwebs and spooky noises didn't scare him.

The baby from two houses down

started to cry. Jigsaw blew sweet
pony breath on him. Soon the baby
was quiet again.

"Jigsaw's so helpful," Kiera said.

"Like one of the big kids," Fran
said.

Jody said, "I bet he'd be a great
babysitter!"

After the party Jody, Fran, and
Kiera led Jigsaw home.

"Tomorrow Tish comes," Kiera
said.

They all looked at Jigsaw. "I hope he's all right," Jody said.

"He's all right," Fran said. "He has to be."

CHAPTER TEN
Tish

The next afternoon Tish came.
Kiera, Fran, and Jody took her out
to meet Jigsaw.

"What a great little pony!" Tish

said. "You've made a nice barn for him. So what's the problem?"

"He doesn't like to keep going fast," Fran said. She told Tish about the barrel racing.

"He doesn't like to keep jumping either," Kiera said. She told Tish about the beanpoles.

"That could be him, or it could be you," Tish said. "Radish taught you more about slowing ponies down than about keeping them going. But let's check Jigsaw out."

Tish felt Jigsaw's ribs and said, *"Hmm."* Fran and Kiera looked at each other.

She listened to his heartbeats and frowned. Mr. and Mrs. Shaw held hands.

She took out a tiny flashlight and flashed it in each of his eyes. "Ah," she said. Jody twisted her fingers together.

Now Tish opened Jigsaw's mouth. She looked inside.

"Oh, my," she said. "My goodness!"

Now Fran and Kiera held hands. They didn't really mean to. It just happened. Mrs. Shaw put one arm around Jody's shoulders.

Tish let Jigsaw close his mouth. She turned.

"The good news," she said, "is that Jigsaw is a very healthy pony for his age. You are taking wonderful care of him."

"What's the not-so-good news?" Mr. Shaw asked.

"The not-so-good news," Tish said, "is that Jigsaw is a *very* old pony."

"How old?" Fran asked.

Tish said, "From the looks of his teeth, about thirty-five. And that means you can't ask him to do too much work."

"How much is too much?" Kiera asked.

"Jigsaw's been telling you," Tish said. "Three jumps in a row is too much. Galloping around three barrels is too much. He can go for short gallops or slow rides that are a little longer. He can jump over one or two jumps. But that's it."

Fran looked at Kiera. Nobody else, not even Jody, understood what she was feeling.

Kiera looked back at Fran. Fran was the only person in the world who knew how she felt.

Jigsaw was old. Too old for barrel racing. Too old for jumping. When they'd dreamed of a pony, Fran and Kiera had dreamed of fast gallops and daring leaps. They had dreamed of long rides. They had dreamed of blue ribbons.

Those dreams were over, and now they had worries.

Fran asked, "Will he—"

Kiera asked, "Is he going to—"

"He'll live a long time," Tish said. "Especially if he gets good care." She smiled sadly and shook her head. "But maybe you won't want to keep him since he can't do everything you want. Lots of people wouldn't."

Fran put her arms around Jigsaw's neck. "*We're* not like that!"

"We like Jigsaw as a *person*," Kiera said. She hugged Jigsaw's neck, too.

Her arms wrapped around Fran's,
and Fran's wrapped around hers.

Fran said, "Jigsaw's not the kind of
pony you do things *on*—"

Kiera said, "That's right. He's the
kind of pony you do things *with*!"

"He's our friend," Jody said. She
kissed his ears.

"More like a member of the
family," said Mr. Shaw, sneaking an
apple out of his pocket.

"He's a great neighbor," said the
baby's mother. She'd come over to
see if something was wrong.

"-igsaw!" squealed the baby.

Jigsaw tickled the baby with his whiskers. This was turning into another party. More neighbors were crossing the street.

The telephone rang, and Mrs. Shaw answered it. "Tish is right—" she said. "He's fine, just older than we—" The person she was talking to didn't let her finish a single sentence.

Jigsaw ate Mr. Shaw's apple. He breathed appley breath on Jody. He leaned into the hugs Kiera and Fran were giving him.

It wasn't easy. The hugs were coming from two sides at once. But Jigsaw did it.

He really could do anything.